The Tale of
THREE
TREES

A Lion Children's Book
an imprint of
Lion Hudson plc
Wilkinson House, Jordan Hill Road
Oxford, OX2 8DR
www.lionhudson.com
ISBN 978 0 7459 6920 6

First edition 1989
This abridged mini edition 2009
This printing August 2009
10 9 8 7 6 5 4 3 2 1 0

A catalogue record for this book is available
from the British Library

Typeset in 14/18 OldClaude
Printed and bound in China
by Printplus Ltd

The Tale of
THREE
TREES

A Traditional Folktale

Retold by Angela Elwell Hunt

Illustrations by Tim Jonke

LION
CHILDREN'S

Once upon a mountaintop, three trees dreamed of what they wanted to become when they grew up.

"I want to hold treasure," the first tree said. "I will be the most beautiful treasure chest in the whole world!"

"I want to be a strong sailing ship," the second tree said.

"I will be the strongest ship in the world."

"I don't want to leave this mountaintop at all," the third tree said. "I want to grow so tall that when people look at me they will raise their eyes to heaven and think of God. I will be the tallest tree in the world!"

One day three woodcutters climbed the mountain.

With a swoop of the first man's axe, the first tree fell.

With a swish of the second man's axe, the second tree fell.

With a slash of the third man's axe, the third tree fell.

The first tree rejoiced when the woodcutter brought him to a carpenter's shop, but the busy carpenter was not thinking about treasure chests. Instead his work-worn hands fashioned the tree into a feed box for animals.

The second tree smiled when the woodcutter took him to a shipyard, but no mighty sailing ships were built that day. Instead the once-strong tree was made into a simple fishing boat.

The third tree was confused when the woodcutter cut her into strong beams and left her in a lumberyard.

"What happened?" the once-tall tree wondered. "All I ever wanted to do was point to God."

Many, many days
and nights passed.
The three trees
nearly forgot their
dreams.

But one night
golden starlight
poured over the
first tree as a young
woman placed her
newborn baby in the
feed box.

And suddenly the
first tree knew he
was holding the
greatest treasure in
the world.

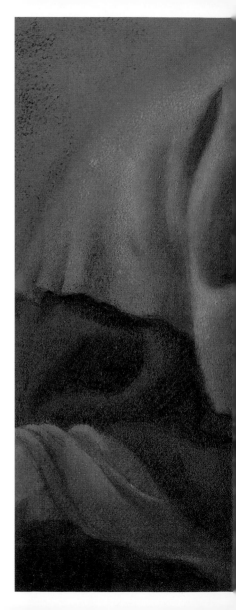

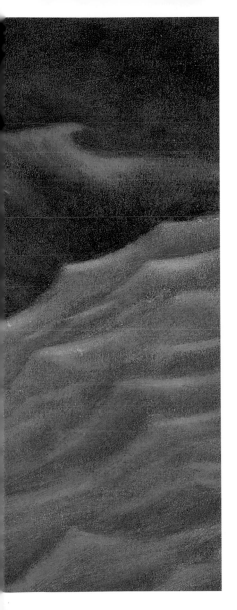

One evening a tired traveller and his friends crowded into the old fishing boat.

When a storm arose, the second tree shuddered. But when the traveller stretched out his hand, and said, "Peace," the storm stopped.

And suddenly the second tree knew he was carrying the King of heaven and earth.

One Friday morning, the third tree was startled when her beams were yanked from the woodpile.

She shivered when she was dragged through an angry crowd. She shuddered when soldiers nailed a man's hands to her.

She felt ugly and harsh and cruel.

But on Sunday morning when the sun rose and the earth trembled with joy beneath her, the third tree knew God's love had changed everything.

It had made the first tree beautiful.

It had made the second tree strong.

And every time people thought of the third tree, they would think of God.